Edward
- and -
Annie

Edward and Annie: A Penguin Adventure

© 2022 Thomas Nelson

Tommy Nelson, PO Box 141000, Nashville, TN 37214

Published in Nashville, Tennessee, by Tommy Nelson. Tommy Nelson is an imprint of Thomas Nelson. Thomas Nelson is a registered trademark of HarperCollins Christian Publishing, Inc.

Tommy Nelson titles may be purchased in bulk for educational, business, fundraising, or sales promotional use. For information, please email SpecialMarkets@ThomasNelson.com.

ISBN 978-1-4002-2830-0 (eBook)
ISBN 978-1-4002-2828-7 (HC)

Library of Congress Cataloging-in-Publication Data

Names: Rivadeneira, Caryn Dahlstrand, author. | Tanis, Katy, illustrator.
Title: Edward and Annie: a penguin adventure / by Caryn Rivadeneira; illustrated by Katy Tanis.
Description: Nashville, TN: Thomas Nelson, [2021] | Audience: Ages 4-8. | Summary: When Chicago's Shedd Aquarium closes down during the Covid-19 pandemic, animal care specialist Kai takes two penguins on a tour of the aquarium, meeting various lake, ocean, river, and reef animals.
Identifiers: LCCN 2021033672 (print) | LCCN 2021033673 (ebook) | ISBN 9781400228287 (hardcover) | ISBN 9781400228300 (epub)
Subjects: LCSH: John G. Shedd Aquarium--Juvenile fiction. | Penguins--Juvenile fiction. | Aquatic animals--Juvenile fiction. | CYAC: John G. Shedd Aquarium--Fiction. | Penguins--Fiction. | Aquatic animals--Fiction. | LCGFT: Picture books.
Classification: LCC PZ10.3.R515 Ed 2021 (print) | LCC PZ10.3.R515 (ebook) | DDC [E]--dc23
LC record available at https://lccn.loc.gov/2021033672
LC ebook record available at https://lccn.loc.gov/2021033673

Written by Caryn Rivadeneira

Illustrated by Katy Tanis

Printed in South Korea

22 23 24 25 26 SHW 6 5 4 3 2 1

Mfr: SHW / Seoul, South Korea / February 2022 / PO #12034411

Edward
- and -
Annie

A Penguin Adventure

by **Caryn Rivadeneira**

illustrated by **Katy Tanis**

in partnership with
Shedd Aquarium

One day at the giant Shedd Aquarium on the shores of the great Lake Michigan, a rockhopper penguin named Annie shook herself awake. Then she fluffed her feathers, just as she did every time she woke up.

Except this time wasn't like every other time.

This time *something* was different.

Annie quickly looked around her home.
But nothing seemed wrong.
　Edward was napping in their big rocky nest.
Normal.

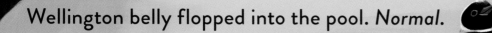

Wellington belly flopped into the pool. *Normal.*

Kai, the penguin caretaker, dropped lavender sprigs and new rocks for nests. *Normal.*

So what's different? Annie wondered.

Annie poked Edward with her pink toe. *Edward,* Annie said. *Wake up! Something is different.*

Edward popped up. *That's exciting!* Edward said. *Different can be fun!*

Before Annie could disagree, Kai walked up to Edward and Annie.
"Hello, loves!" Kai said. "Glad you're awake. I have a surprise."

A *surprise?* Edward wiggled a yellow eyebrow at Annie.

Kai scratched Annie's head.
Edward waddled up for a snuggle.
  "We're going on an adventure!" Kai said.
  An adventure! Edward hopped toward Annie.
That is different!

Annie was feeling cautious about the adventure.
Still, Kai always pet them, brought them rocks,
and fed them herring and krill. So when
Kai said, "Follow me!" Edward and Annie
waddled behind.

"It's time to meet your neighbors," Kai said. Ahead, the sleek, brown bodies of two sea otters shimmered in the water. "When Cooper and Watson were tiny pups, they lost their moms off the coast of California," Kai said. "They were both rescued and given a home here at Shedd."

Edward and Annie watched the otters somersault and play tag. As the otters raced past them, Watson did an extra spin right in front of Annie.

"Time to move on," Kai said. "Goodbye, Cooper! Goodbye, Watson!" Edward and Annie raised their flippers. *Waving goodbye to rescued otters. This is different!* Annie thought.

Ahead, beluga whales tumbled
and turned in the dusky-blue water.

"Listen," Kai said.

Edward and Annie waddled closer. The whales chirped and cooed. A smaller, creamy beluga slid up to the glass.

"Hello, Annik!" Kai said.

Annik bobbed his melon-shaped head. Edward waved a wing. Annie shook her top feathers. Then Annik swam away—backward!

Singing whales that swim backward. That's different! Annie thought as she watched the belugas float up to the tippy top of their pool.

"We're going up too," Kai said. "And you two need some exercise! Let's take the stairs."

How? Edward asked.

*We're rock*hoppers, *silly*, Annie said.

So Edward and Annie hopped
and hopped
and hopped.

Edward and Annie hopped up the very last step. *Whew!*

"Time for a rest and a snack," Kai said. Kai plopped a tiny herring into Edward's beak and another into Annie's open mouth.

Around them, blue lights sparkled. Angelfish, butterfly fish, cow-nosed rays, and bonnethead sharks swam by.

"Here's Nickel." Kai pointed at a green sea turtle. A deep scar ran across her shell. "She got hurt by a boat. Now she can't swim well enough to live in the Caribbean Sea. But she has a safe home here!"

Nickel swam in a little loop, waving one of her front flippers at them.

Edward turned to share this good news with Annie. But she was gone. *Oh no! That's different!*

AMAZON
rising

"Where did Annie go?" Kai asked.
"Let's see if she's in the Amazon."
    Tree branches and vines stretched across the ceiling.
Pools of glimmering green water lined the walls. Inside
swam piranhas, tiger rays, and matamata turtles.

Kai and Edward found Annie peering through the glass of the pools. Giant arapaima slid past. Their scales glinted silver and red.

A person Annie didn't recognize lowered a pole into the water. The arapaima nosed the end of the pole. Then the person tossed a piece of fish. The arapaima opened his mouth so fast that it made a loud pop as he snapped up the food.

Their person makes mealtime fun too! Annie thought.

Edward, Annie said, *these fish are so fun to watch! Meeting all these animals from oceans and rivers and lakes is amazing.*

Maybe that's why people like visiting us, Edward said.

Annie teetered on her webbed feet. *That's it*, she said. *There are no people here! That's what is different! But what will happen without the visitors?*

"One more stop," Kai said.

Just then, elevator doors chimed. Edward and Annie hopped in after Kai. The elevator went down,

down,

down.

One family per elevator

Ding!

"Here we are," Kai said. "At Wild Reef."

Sunlight streaked through deep blue water. Yellow and orange fins sparkled like confetti among sleek, gray fish that glided past.

It's like we're at the bottom of the ocean, Annie said.

Edward and Annie hopped toward the porcupine fish and sandbar sharks, clown fish and spotted wobbegongs. Suddenly, what looked like a flat shark floated out from the rocks.

"It's Lucy, the white-spotted guitarfish," Kai said. "She stays close to the bottom of the ocean."

Edward! Annie said in surprise. *Lucy doesn't have a mouth!*
Just then, Lucy swam to the side and gave Edward and Annie a big smile.
"Lucy's mouth is on the underside of her body," Kai said. "She picks up crab and clamshells from the ocean floor."
An underside smile, Annie thought. *That's different too! Good different.*

"Our adventure is over for today," Kai said. "I hope you enjoyed exploring! Getting out and flapping our wings is good for everyone. Soon the aquarium will be open again, and things will be back to normal."

Normal? Annie questioned Edward. *Does that mean the people will come back? Will normal feel* different *then?*

Sometimes normal is good too, Edward said. *Don't worry—we'll be together.* Edward nuzzled his beak into Annie's feathers.

Annie thought of her nest with Edward. She thought of the swimming pool with Wellington and the rest of her penguin friends. And the delicious fish Kai brought every day. She knew she was safe. Normal *was* pretty good.

But different can be exciting! Annie said. *Especially when I'm with you and Kai.*

As Kai led them home, the two penguins dreamed of new adventures in the giant Shedd Aquarium on the shores of the great Lake Michigan.

About Shedd Aquarium

Shedd Aquarium in Chicago is home to more than 1,500 species. These creatures include fish, amphibians, birds, marine mammals, snakes, insects, corals, and many more. Shedd gives these animals a safe (and fun!) place to live.

The people who take care of the animals are called *animal care specialists*. These animal experts provide healthy food, medical services, safe habitats, and lots of care to the animals.

Animal care specialists also do activities called *enrichment exercises* with the animals. These activities give the animals' brains and bodies exercise—just like how practicing math and playing outside keep your brain and body healthy. The exercises also help the animals practice for when they need to take medicine or visit the veterinarian. Animal care specialists use fun activities the animals already know to keep them calm while the medical team cares for them. Plus, enrichment exercises help people and animals bond. The animals make friends with their care specialists and learn to trust them.

Enrichment exercises can be simple things such as target training at feeding—like the care specialist did with the arapaima. Or enrichment exercises can be special adventures—like outings to explore new places. That's what happened in 2020 when the aquarium briefly closed to the public during the COVID-19 pandemic. The penguin care specialists took Edward and Annie and their penguin friends on explorations through the empty aquarium. The penguins met many other animals living there, and everyone had a blast making new friends!

Caring for the animals at Shedd Aquarium helps us care for animals in the wild. The more we know and learn about these wonderful animals, the better we can protect those that swim in the world's rivers, oceans, seas, and lakes—and the ones who hop on its rocky shores.